A SPECIAL THANKS
to Barnaby Dallas for helping me co-write *The Glory Express*.
His enthusiasm and passion for the Hubcap Kids' family
will always be appreciated.

THIS BOOK IS DEDICATED
to my wife, Marianne, and daughters Lauren and Ashley,
and to my parents, and brothers Joe and Gary. Thank you
all for your love and encouragement.

*Each man should give what he has decided in his heart to give, not reluctantly
or under compulsion, for God loves a cheerful giver. And God is able to make
all grace abound to you, so that in all things at all times, having all that
you need, you will abound in every good work.*
*2 Corinthians 9:7-8*

Copyright © 2000 by Pat Sunseri
Published in 2000 by
Broadman & Holman Publishers
Nashville, Tennessee

**Library of Congress Cataloging-in-Publication Data**

Sunseri, Pat, 1955-
    The Glory Express / story and illustrations by Pat Sunseri.
        p. cm. -- (Hubcap kids adventures)
    Summary: When two children give all their savings to help others in need, it inspires
    the other residents of Hubcap Flats to find ways to help as well.
    ISBN 0-8054-2056-8
    [1. Generosity--Fiction.] I. Title.

PZ7.S958273 G1 2000
[E]--dc21
                                                                                            99-054544

Scripture quotations are from the Holy Bible, New International Version,
copyright 1973, 1978, 1984 by International Bible Society.

# Hubcap Kids Adventures

# The Glory Express

## story and illustrations by Pat Sunseri

Steam billowed from the smokestack as the bells rang to announce Glory Express' arrival to Hubcap Flats. For forty days, Hubcaps rode the Glory Express from town to town to gather goods to help those in need across the land. Usually when Glory Express rolled into Hubcap Flats, the freight cars were overflowing with donated food, gifts, and other goods. But there was something different about the Glory Express this year. The train was empty.

Hubcaps, tired from his long journey, was greeted by Axle, Ethyl, and a few of the Hubcap kids. They all wanted to know why Glory was empty.

Hubcaps stood on an empty flat car and said, "It's been a hard year and people don't have as much to give. There are many people who count on us and now is the time we need to come together and work to fill Glory up with supplies."

Hubcaps, determined to fill Glory with food and supplies, went to Ethyl's diner for a bowl of soup and some biscuits so he would have the strength to continue his journey. Hubcaps looked up from his soup and said, "Glory needs more coal. I'll be gone for three days. When I get back, I'll think of a way to fill Glory up."

"But why get more coal if there is nothing to put in old Glory?" Axle asked.

"We can't give up. We have to do whatever we can, no matter how hopeless it may seem. People need us," Hubcaps said.

After his meal, Hubcaps was leaving the diner when Half-Inch and Nine-Sixteenths handed Hubcaps an old can.

"What is this, kids?" Hubcaps said.

"Mr. Hubcaps," Half-Inch said, "we heard what you said back at old Glory and we want to help. We've been putting our money in this old can to save for a toy train. Please take our money and buy something to help fill Glory. We know it isn't much, but it's all we have."

Hubcaps was overwhelmed with their generosity and invited them to go back to the train station to show them how far their help would go.

In the train station, Hubcaps said, "You two have really made me proud. I know how hard it is for people to help when times are tough, but you two gave everything you could."

The boys gathered around Hubcaps as he said, "Here is a map of all the stops Glory makes. Every year we reach out to those across the land, and it is good deeds like yours that allows the Glory to share these gifts with others. I'm on my way to get more coal, and when I get back we'll find a way to fill old Glory."

The next morning as Hubcaps was off to get more coal, Axle, who had been outside the diner and seen Half-Inch and Nine-Sixteenths give Hubcaps the can, called a special meeting outside the clubhouse. "If Half-Inch and Nine-Sixteenths can make a sacrifice, so can we. We should all try to help Hubcaps fill Glory," Axle said.

Within no time, Hubcap Flats was buzzing with excitement. There was a lot of work to be done, but they would all work together to try and fill the Glory Express.

Molly Bolt, Clutch, and Woody went out with Axle to post flyers and signs around the region to explain the urgency of the care boxes.

Ethyl and some of the kids began to gather sacks of wheat and grains to take to Glory Express. Half-Inch and Nine-Sixteenths, who were now even more excited to help Hubcaps, showed up with a wagon filled with corn.

Meanwhile, Hubcaps, inspired by Half-Inch and Nine-Sixteenths' act of kindness, went to the coal mine and worked night and day getting enough coal for the Glory Express to take another trip.

When Axle and his friends finished putting up signs for the care boxes, they came back to help Ethyl gather clothes and blankets. Molly Bolt cut scraps of rags and Ethyl sewed them together to make wonderful blankets to load on Glory Express.

After three days, Hubcaps returned to Hubcaps Flats with a full load of coal. He couldn't believe his eyes when he gazed at the docks and saw full bins of food, clothing, and goods. When Hubcaps asked where everything came from, Axle said "We all worked together and people from all over answered our call for the Hubcaps donation drive."

"But where is everyone else?" Hubcaps asked.

"That's the second surprise," Axle replied.

Everyone was gathered at the Hubcap picnic grounds for a celebration. All the kids were standing around a brand new train set that looked just like the Glory Express.

"Who's it for?" Half-Inch asked.

"For both of you!" Axle said. "Thank you for showing us the true gift of giving. It's your turn now to ride the rails."

Hubcaps turned to Half-Inch and Nine-Sixteenths and said "Sometimes the best gifts come from small packages."